ISBN 0-8114-9303-2

7 8 9 01 00

Produced by Mega-Books of New York, Inc.
Design and Art Direction by Michaelis/Carpelis Design Assoc.

Cover illustration: Ken Spencer

GRAVE DISCOVERY

by Judy Katschke

interior illustrations by
Gary Undercuffler

STECK-VAUGHN
ELEMENTARY · SECONDARY · ADULT · LIBRARY

A Harcourt Company

www.steck-vaughn.com

CHAPTER ONE

"It's the monster!" yelled Mario Cruz as he jumped onto the desk. "It's alive! It's alive!"

Mr. Dixon stared up at Mario. "Yeah, you'll do," he said, folding a paper airplane. "See Crystal on the way out. She'll give you your costume and your torch. You can start right away."

Mario couldn't believe it! He had gotten a summer job at the Castle of Fear! The Castle was the coolest, creepiest amusement park around.

Mario ran to the locker room. He changed into his Igor costume. Mario knew Igor was the "right hand" of Doctor Frankenstein. He also knew

Igor was a hunchback and that he limped.

Mario made sure his cape was tied and his hunch was in place. Then he headed for his work station.

"This place is awesome!" he thought as he limped through the Castle. The cobwebs looked real. So did the blood dripping down the walls.

"How do they do that?" Mario wondered.

Mario peeked into a nearby coffin. He saw a girl with long, red hair inside.

"Cute," Mario said under his breath. The girl in the coffin winked at him.

Mario smiled. "I think I'm going to like it here," he thought.

Mario wandered into his dungeon. He looked over the room. Then he went straight to the tall, dark box leaning against the wall.

"Anybody home?" he called, opening the box's carved lid.

"Hey! Don't blow my cover!" snapped

a voice from within the box. Mario jumped back. Inside the box was a skeleton lying between sharp spikes.

"Sorry about that," Mario told the angry skeleton.

Suddenly a man in a T-shirt and jeans stepped out of the shadows.

"Who are you?" asked Mario.

"My name's Pete," answered the man. "I'm the prop master."

Mario grabbed Pete's arm. "Master! Master!" he cried, playing Igor.

Pete grinned. "Very funny," he said.

"Do you do the special effects, like making the floors tilt and the lights turn on and off?" asked Mario.

Pete nodded.

"You do amazing work," Mario said. "This place is just as cool as a horror movie!"

"I wish it was one," mumbled Pete.

"Have you ever worked in the movies?" Mario asked.

Pete shook his head. "I never finished

high school. A job at this place is as good as it gets for me."

Mario reached out to shake Pete's hand. "I'm Mario Cruz. I'm working here for the summer."

"Just keep your hands off the gizmos, Mario," warned Pete.

"Oh yes, Master, yes," Mario called as he limped away.

Mario's day wore on, but the fun of being Igor began to wear off. His cape made him sweat. His ears hurt from the visitors' screams. His eyes hurt from their camera flashes.

Mario saw a woman walking alone in the hall. He limped over to her.

"Do you find me gruesome?" he demanded.

"What I want to find is the snack bar," she answered.

"Go to the gallows and *hang* a left," Mario directed her.

Suddenly Mario heard heavy footsteps. He swung around. Coming

toward him were four figures wearing black hoods and long capes. In their hands were huge, gleaming axes.

Mario whistled as they marched by. "Now *they* are cool. Way cool!"

CHAPTER TWO

"You've been Igor for just one day. Now you want a transfer?" asked Mr. Dixon.

"It's just that I know I'd make a great executioner," Mario explained.

"Get to work, Mario," said Mr. Dixon. He began folding a paper airplane.

"I guess that means no," Mario mumbled to himself.

All of a sudden the door to Mr. Dixon's office burst open. "What can I do for you?" Crystal was asking the girl who rushed in.

"My gold chain is gone," the girl gasped. She was almost out of breath. "When the lights went out, somebody

ripped the whole chain off of my neck!"

Mario saw a fake noose on a prop shelf. He held it up. "Is this it?" he asked the girl.

Mr. Dixon crumpled up his airplane. He looked straight at Mario. "I said, get to work."

Mario slipped out the door and headed for his dungeon. On the way there, a mummy ran over to him. "What now?" Mario wondered.

"Mario," the mummy pleaded. "Could you cover for me in the Castle hall? I'm starting to unravel!"

Mario laughed. "Sure," he said. He

turned and entered the large, musty hall. He was about to hide behind a statue so he could really scare visitors. But suddenly the lights went out.

"Give me a break, Pete!" Mario hissed. "I can't see where I'm going!"

As Mario waited in the dark he heard the sound of heavy footsteps again.

Mario remembered the torch he was carrying. He turned it on in time to see the four executioners. They were marching along in single file.

Mario grinned. He decided to limp after them, Igor-style. He followed the executioners all the way to the Castle's secret tunnel.

"What are they doing in there?" wondered Mario. From the opening of the secret tunnel he could hear the executioners speaking.

"What did you get this time?" asked a squeaky voice.

"Cash and credit cards," answered a deep voice. "That guy had no idea his wallet was being stolen."

The executioners were talking about ripping off the visitors! Mario strained to hear more.

"Good old Pete," said the squeaky voice. "He knows just when to turn off the lights!"

Mario fell back against the wall. "Pete? No way!" he whispered to himself.

Mario thought about telling Mr. Dixon what he had heard, but he figured his boss wouldn't believe him. Mr. Dixon would just think the story was sour grapes on Mario's part.

Suddenly, Mario's torch slipped from his hand.

"Great!" thought Mario. He rolled his eyes as the torch bumped noisily onto the floor.

The executioners rushed from the tunnel. With their hoods over their faces, they surrounded Mario.

"How did you know we were in

there, Igor?" asked the tallest executioner.

Mario shrugged. "Just a *hunch*," he suggested.

Another executioner picked up an ax. "Stay out of this, funny boy, or you'll be a *real* cutup!"

"N-no problem!" Mario gasped. He picked up his torch and ran off down the hall.

"We'll be watching you, Igor!" the executioners shouted after him.

Mario brushed away cobwebs as he ran. Whizzing around a corner, he crashed right into Pete.

"Hey, what's wrong, Igor? You look like you've seen a ghost," Pete joked.

CHAPTER THREE

When he arrived at work the next day, Mario was worried. If the Castle of Fear got a bad name, no one would come. If no one came, there wouldn't be a summer job for him. Mario decided to find out who the executioners were. He walked slowly through the Castle, looking around.

"Gotcha!" he cried as he yanked the hood off an executioner's head. Long, red hair tumbled down. It was the girl from the coffin.

"Do you like my new costume?" she asked Mario. "Mr. Dixon has us change parts sometimes."

A nearby Dracula saw the puzzled

look on Mario's face. "Maybe Mr. Dixon *vants* some new blood!" joked the vampire.

So all the parts were changed around! Mario would never find the thieves now.

"Starting today, you're the Castle's undertaker," announced Mr. Dixon when Mario punched in for work.

"But you know how much I want to

be an executioner," Mario reminded Mr. Dixon.

"Yeah, but until then, you've got the graveyard shift." Mr. Dixon reached for a shovel. He handed it to Mario. "You *dig*?" he asked.

Mario trudged off to the locker room. He exchanged his hunch for a pair of ratty overalls.

"Bor-r-ring," mumbled Mario as he left the locker room. He looked at the other kids in their new costumes. Who was watching him now? The warlock? The phantom? Mario looked into the coffin as he passed by. A new girl was lying inside. Could she be the thief with the squeaky voice?

"Hey," whispered Mario. "How do you like being dead?"

"It's a *living*," hissed the girl. "Now, go away!" Mario wasn't sure he knew the voice.

Just as Mario was nearing the Castle's exit, the floor began to shake and tilt.

"Pete's at it again," thought Mario. Soon the lights were flickering so fast Mario couldn't see who was running by. Someone shoved him. He tumbled to the floor.

"Hey, watch it!" Mario shouted as he tried to get up. The floor was still tilting and herds of screaming people were jumping over him. Mario was about to call for help when the floor finally stopped moving and the lights stopped flickering.

A girl laughed. "That was so excellent!" she shouted to her friends.

"Wait a minute!" shouted someone else. "My wallet is gone!"

Mario shook his head. "Here we go again," he groaned.

By late afternoon Mario already hated his new part. The graveyard was in the backyard of the Castle. Hardly any visitors came by. To make things worse, Pete had warned him not to dig into any of the graves.

"Whoever heard of a gravedigger who doesn't dig?" Mario mumbled. In a huff, he jabbed his shovel into a lumpy grave. He jumped when the shovel hit something in the dirt.

Mario bent down. He quickly uncovered a small bundle wrapped in a garbage bag. Inside were wallets, credit cards, watches, and jewelry. This loot was just the evidence he needed to go to Mr. Dixon!

"No wonder Pete told me not to dig

into the graves," thought Mario. "He's in on this ripoff thing, all right!"

Mario didn't want to take any chances. He tossed the bundle back into the grave and kicked dirt over it. Then he hid his shovel behind a tombstone. He would come back at night when everybody except Mr. Dixon was gone. Then he would show Mr. Dixon the loot.

Mario wandered around the Castle grounds pretending nothing was wrong. When he reached his locker, his blood froze. Sprayed on the door in red paint were the words WE'RE WATCHING YOU, FUNNY BOY!

CHAPTER FOUR

The Castle of Fear was even creepier at night than during the day. Shadows swept over the graveyard. Mario quickly got his shovel and dug into the grave. But now it was empty!

"I've got to go to Mr. Dixon anyway," Mario decided.

Mario trudged up the Castle steps and pushed open the great door. "Anybody around?" he called as he walked in.

Suddenly the heavy door slammed shut behind him. Mario whizzed around. Facing him were four figures wearing capes and hoods and carrying huge axes.

"We warned you to stay out of this,

hunchback," snapped the squeaky voice.

"I'm just *Igor* to please," Mario joked nervously as he stepped back.

Just as the executioners were closing in on Mario, a dusty net dropped down over them.

"Hey! What's going on?" they yelled.

Mario flew down a nearby staircase and headed for Doctor Frankenstein's lab. He hid behind a table of glass jars.

"He's in here!" shouted the deep voice.

Mario rolled his eyes. "I'm history," he groaned under his breath.

Just then, a black mist began to ooze from the jars. Soon the whole lab was buried in thick fog. Mario escaped. "Is the Castle of Fear really spooked?" he wondered.

Mario stopped at another staircase. The sign was marked BELL TOWER. He began to climb.

"I'm moving up in the world," Mario thought as he reached the top. He shuddered when he heard the

thunder of feet below.

The executioners were following Mario into the tower! There seemed to be no way out for Mario. Or was there?

Mario stared at the giant, rusty bell swinging above him. He took a deep breath. Then he jumped for the bell.

"He's crazy!" shrieked the squeaky voice as Mario swung on the bell.

"How long can I keep this up?" Mario wondered. The axes swayed below him. Through the blaring bell clangs Mario heard a creak. Suddenly the bell started moving down!

A trap door in the tower floor opened. Mario held on tightly as the bell dropped down through the door.

The bell hit the ground. Mario jumped off and made a dash for the back door of the Castle. The heavy door slammed shut behind him. Then there was a loud click. Mario breathed a sigh of relief when he heard fists pounding on the other side. The door was locked!

Mario collapsed in the graveyard. When he opened his eyes, Pete was standing over him.

"I was working in my shop when those kids ganged up on you," Pete explained. "So I decided to have a

little fun and stop them cold." Pete chuckled.

"Thanks a lot," said Mario. "I was beginning to think this was a real *dead-end* job!"

"Yeah. And look at what they dropped," Pete added. He threw the bag of loot at Mario. "I knew those four kids were trouble!"

Mario was glad he was wrong about Pete. But he still wanted to know why he couldn't dig into the graves.

"I'll show you," said Pete. He pulled out a remote-control switch and zapped it at a tombstone. A mechanical corpse popped out of a grave.

Mario grinned. "You really do some amazing work," he said to Pete.

"Piece of cake," answered Pete. "Now, let's call Mr. Dixon . . . and the police."

The next morning the Castle of Fear was buzzing with news of the executioners' arrests. And everyone wanted to talk to Mario. Even Mr. Dixon

called him to the office for a talk.

Mario gulped. "I'm getting the *ax*?" he asked. He couldn't believe it.

"No," answered Mr. Dixon. "I'm *giving* you the ax. I'm making you an executioner!" Mr. Dixon laughed and handed Mario an ax.

Mario shook his head. "Thanks, but right now that's just about the last thing I want to be."

Mr. Dixon was puzzled. "Well, what part do you want?" he asked Mario.

Mario hunched his shoulder. "Maybe we could discuss my career *ghouls*?"

Mr. Dixon tossed a paper airplane at Mario. "Get to work, Igor!" he said.

Later in the morning Mario had another surprise. Pete told him he had decided to go back to school.

"After the show I put on last night, I figured the movies could use a guy like me," said Pete proudly.

"That's great!" Mario replied. "If you ever make a new Frankenstein movie,"

Mario grinned, "Call me, Master."

Pete laughed and walked on. Mario crept up to a little boy standing by the Castle fountain.

"Do you find me gruesome?" he demanded.

The boy shrieked and ran off.

"And this place could sure use a guy like me!" Mario decided.